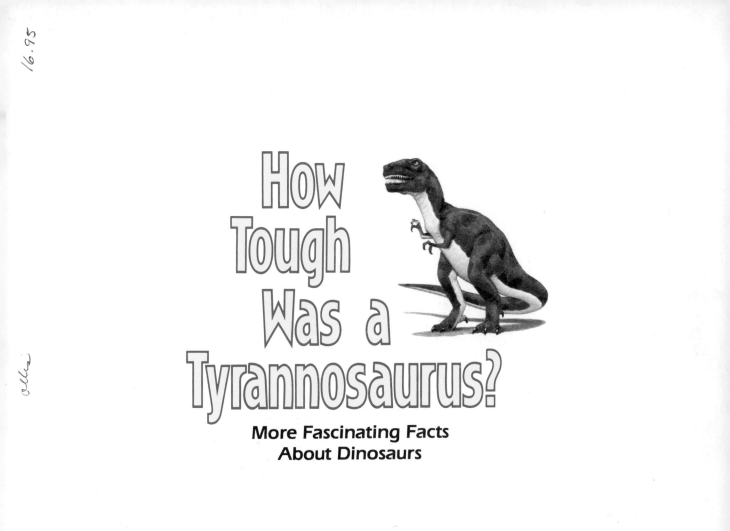

How Tough Was a Tyrannosaurus?

**More Fascinating Facts
About Dinosaurs**

A Grosset & Dunlap **ALL ABOARD BOOK**™

How Tough

Text copyright © 1989 by Paul C. Sereno. Illustrations copyright © 1987 by
Courtney Studios. All rights reserved. Published by Grosset & Dunlap, Inc., a
member of The Putnam & Grosset Group, New York. ALL ABOARD BOOKS
is a trademark of The Putnam & Grosset Group. THE LITTLE ENGINE THAT
COULD and engine design are trademarks of Platt & Munk, Publishers.
Published simultaneously in Canada. Printed in the U.S.A. Library of
Congress Catalog Card Number: 88-81180 ISBN 0-448-19116-4
E F G H I J

Was a Tyrannosaurus?

More Fascinating Facts About Dinosaurs

By Dr. Paul C. Sereno
Department of Anatomy
University of Chicago

Grosset & Dunlap, Publishers

When did dinosaurs live on earth?

Dinosaurs lived during the period that scientists call the Mesozoic (mez-uh-ZOH-ick) era, or "middle" age. It lasted nearly 160 million years, from about 225 million years ago to about 65 million years ago.

In comparison, human beings appeared on earth very recently—only one-and-a-half million years ago. That was long after the last of these great beasts died.

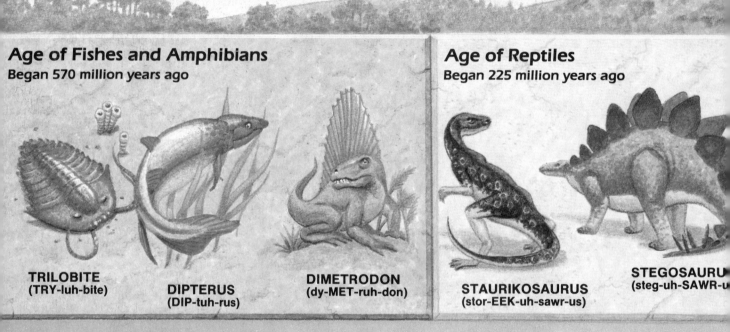

Age of Fishes and Amphibians
Began 570 million years ago

Age of Reptiles
Began 225 million years ago

TRILOBITE
(TRY-luh-bite)

DIPTERUS
(DIP-tuh-rus)

DIMETRODON
(dy-MET-ruh-don)

STAURIKOSAURUS
(stor-EEK-uh-sawr-us)

STEGOSAURU
(steg-uh-SAWR-u

TRICERATOPS
(try-SAIR-uh-tops)

Did all the dinosaurs live at the same time?

Dinosaurs lived on earth for many millions of years, but no one kind of dinosaur existed for the entire time. Fierce *Tyrannosaurus* (tuh-ran-uh-SAWR-us), for example, appeared only near the very end of the dinosaur age. Many other dinosaurs had already appeared and become extinct—died out.

4

Which dinosaurs lived the latest?

Tyrannosaurus was one of the last dinosaurs that we know about. Along with the bones of the horned dinosaur *Triceratops* (try-SAIR-uh-tops), those of *Tyrannosaurus* are found in rocks from the very end of the age of dinosaurs.

TYRANNOSAURUS

Age of Mammals
Began 65 million years ago

HYRACOTHERIUM
(hy-rack-uh-THEER-ee-um)

ALTICAMELUS
(ahl-tuh-CAM-uh-lus)

EARLY HUMAN

RANNOSAURUS
ı-ran-uh-SAWR-us)

5

What were the earliest dinosaurs like?

Some of the earliest dinosaurs were flesh-eaters. Others were plant-eaters. They lived in South America and grew to about six feet in length. Many of the later dinosaurs, such as *Tyrannosaurus*, reached much larger sizes.

PISANOSAURUS
(puh-SAN-uh-sawr-us)

What was the earth like when the dinosaurs lived?

The first dinosaurs lived along rivers and in moist forests of tall ferns. The climate in those forests was like that of some forests on earth today. The temperature changed little from season to season. It was generally warm.

Toward the end of the age of dinosaurs, many plants that are common in parks today appeared for the first time. Those plants include grasses, flowering plants, and trees that lose their leaves in winter.

At that time the temperature in northern lands, such as Alaska, was warmer than it is today. That allowed the dinosaurs to spread far to the north on land that is now usually covered with snow.

STAURIKOSAURUS

7

Where did dinosaurs live?

Dinosaurs lived in many places, from forest to desert, just like modern animals do. We find their footprints and nesting sites along ancient riverbeds as well as in huge sand dunes. The dinosaurs we know best lived near rivers and lakes, where their bones were quickly buried in the soft mud at the bottom.

TYRANNOSAURUS

CORYTHOSAURUS
(ko-rith-uh-SAWR-us)

Because the climate of the earth changed over millions of years, some areas that were once forests are now dry deserts. We find dinosaur bones today in places where the climate is very different from when the dinosaurs lived there.

ANKYLOSAURUS
(an-ky-luh-SAWR-us)

ASTRODON
(ASS-tro-don)

PROTOCERATOPS
(pro-to-SAIR-uh-tops)

OVIRAPTOR
(o-vuh-RAP-tor)

9

Did other animals live alongside the dinosaurs?

Fish, frogs, turtles, lizards, and even mouse-sized mammals lived at the same time as the dinosaurs. For hungry meat-eating dinosaurs such as *Tyrannosaurus*, those animals were too small to make a satisfying meal. Some were smaller than a single *Tyrannosaurus* tooth—about six inches long.

PTERANODON
(tuh-RAN-uh-don)

ICHTHYOSAURUS
(ick-thee-uh-SAWR-us)

PTERASPIS
(ter-ASS-pus)

EDMONTOSAURUS
(ed-mon-tuh-SAWR-us)

NEOBATRACHUS
(nee-o-buh-TRACK-us)

YOUNG COMPSOGNATHID
(comp-sug-NA-thid)

ARCHELON
(AR-kuh-lon)

11

Since no people lived when the dinosaurs did, how do we find out about dinosaurs?

All of what we know about dinosaurs comes from the discovery of their bones, teeth, skin, eggs, and footprints. These have been preserved in the ground for millions of years. We call these remains fossils. What dinosaurs ate, how fast dinosaurs ran, how large dinosaurs grew, and when dinosaurs died out, must be answered from examining fossils.

CERATOSAURUS
(sair-at-uh-SAWR-us)

How do people find dinosaur bones?

It would be very difficult to find a dinosaur simply by picking a spot and digging, even if someone else had already found dinosaur bones nearby. The skeleton of a dinosaur is discovered when some part of it is poking out of the ground so that an alert dinosaur hunter can see it.

Who studies dinosaurs?

The people who study dinosaur bones are called paleontologists (pay-lee-on-TAHL-uh-jists). They find and dig up dinosaur bones. They write about their discoveries. They try to understand how one kind of dinosaur is related to another kind.

Paleontologists need to study many other sciences, such as biology (animals and plants) and geology (earth and rocks), in order to understand the bones of dinosaurs.

In what kinds of places are most dinosaurs bones found?

Dinosaur bones are *not* found in jungles, swamps, or forests. They *are* found in dry, barren places such as deserts and badlands, where the soil and plants have been blown away by wind and rain. In those places it is possible to see dinosaur bones sticking out of the ground.

In what part of the world have the most dinosaur bones been found?

The places with the most dinosaur skeletons are the deserts of the western United States and across the Pacific Ocean in the deserts of Asia. In ancient times North America and Asia were connected by a land bridge from Eastern Siberia to Alaska. The dinosaurs were able to move from one continent to another.

Where was the first dinosaur bone found?

The first dinosaur bone on record was found in England in 1677 by a man named Robert Plot, who worked in a small museum. He was the first to draw a picture of a dinosaur bone in a book and explain how unusual the bone was. Because he found only one large leg bone with no other part of the dinosaur skeleton, he thought it belonged to an ancient human giant.

ROBERT PLOT

EDMONTOSAURUS

What is the most complete dinosaur skeleton ever found?

The most complete skeleton is that of a duck-billed dinosaur, *Edmontosaurus* (ed-mon-tuh-SAWR-us). It was found in Wyoming as a "fossil mummy" with a covering of skin.

What is the biggest dinosaur skeleton ever found?

The biggest dinosaur skeleton belongs to *Brachiosaurus* (brak-ee-uh-SAWR-us), a huge plant-eating dinosaur that lived before *Tyrannosaurus*. The skeleton of *Brachiosaurus* is 75 feet long, and the head is lifted more than 40 feet above the ground by its long neck.

BRACHIOSAURUS SKELETON

HUMAN SKELETON

Which dinosaur had the biggest head?

Among land-dwelling animals, the largest head ever found was that of *Triceratops*. Its skull was more than four feet long.

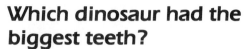

Which dinosaur had the biggest teeth?

The longest teeth—more than six inches—belonged to a *Tyrannosaurus*.

How old did dinosaurs get?

It is easy to tell a dinosaur baby, with its large eyes and head, from an adult. But it is hard to know the exact age of adult dinosaurs. Some may have lived a hundred years.

PROTOCERATOPS

How many different kinds of dinosaurs were there?

There were nearly 500 different kinds of dinosaurs. Some were small and some were large. Some ate plants and others ate meat. Some were very different from each other and others were nearly the same.

APATOSAURUS
(uh-pat-uh-SAWR-us)

EDMONTOSAURUS

COELURUS
(see-LURE-us)

PROTOCERATOPS

For example, *Tyrannosaurus*, which lived in North America, was only slightly different from *Tarbosaurus* (tar-buh-SAWR-us), a large flesh-eating dinosaur that lived in Asia. Both were living at the same time, about 70 million years ago.

TYRANNOSAURUS

STEGOSAURUS

OVIRAPTOR

EUOPLOCEPHALUS
(yu-o-plo-SEF-uh-lus)

Dinosaurs can be divided into two main groups, according to the arrangement of their hip bones. One group had hip bones like a lizard's. We call these saurischians (sore-ISS-kee-anz), or lizard-hipped dinosaurs. This group includes all flesh-eaters, such as *Tyrannosaurus*, and plant-eaters like *Brachiosaurus*, which we call sauropods (SAWR-uh-podz).

"LIZARD HIP"

BRACHIOSAURUS

TYRANNOSAURUS

The other group had a hip arrangement like that of a bird. Dinosaurs in this group are called *ornithischians* (or-nuh-THISS-kee-anz), or bird-hipped dinosaurs. The group includes all the rest of the plant-eaters, such as the horned dinosaur *Triceratops* and the duck-billed dinosaur *Edmontosaurus*.

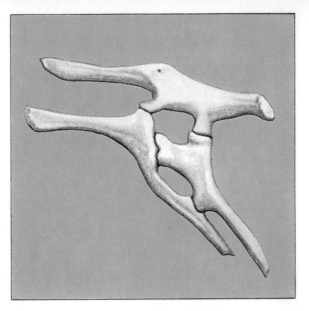

"BIRD HIP"

EDMONTOSAURUS

TRICERATOPS

Which dinosaurs were most common?

The plant-eating dinosaurs were more common than the flesh-eating ones. It was easier to find plants to eat than to catch a fast-running animal. Many plant-eating dinosaurs were needed to provide enough food for a few flesh-eating dinosaurs. So the flesh-eaters never became as widespread as the plant-eaters.

TYRANNOSAURUS

PARASAUROLOPHUS
(par-uh-sawr-AHL-uh-fus)

Were dinosaurs warm-blooded or cold-blooded?

Some dinosaurs were probably warm-blooded, with a high body temperature and an active life, like living mammals and birds. We find footprints that show that some dinosaurs could run very fast.

Other dinosaurs may have been cold-blooded and less active, like lizards and turtles. And some dinosaurs were probably in between.

Could any dinosaurs fly?

No. Birds, which are descended from dinosaurs, are the best living fliers. But no dinosaur could fly, no matter how hard it flapped.

Ancient birds lived among their dinosaur relatives. There were also large creatures called pterosaurs (TER-uh-sawrz) that flew high above the heads of dinosaurs. Their wings were made of a thin sheet of skin instead of the feathers that make up a bird's wings. The largest pterosaur had a wingspan of more than 35 feet—surely the biggest creature ever to fly.

ARCHAEOPTERYX
(ahr-kee-OP-ter-icks)

PTERANODON

Could any dinosaurs swim?

Yes. Dinosaur footprints show that dinosaurs walked in mud and in shallow pools of water. Sometimes they walked into deeper water and began to float so that only the tips of their toes scratched the soft bottom.

ICHTHYOSAURUS

Dinosaurs did not swim in the open seas. The deep water was home to other reptiles that were fast swimmers. Some, like *Ichthyosaurus* (ick-thee-uh-SAWR-us) had a body shaped like a fish, which could move quickly through the water.

How did dinosaurs protect themselves from attack?

Many peaceful plant-eaters were well equipped to ward off the fearsome *Tyrannosaurus*. Some dinosaurs, such as *Ankylosaurus* (an-ky-luh-SAWR-us), were covered by a thick layer of armor and had a large club at the end of their tails. *Stegosaurus*, another armored plant-eating dinosaur, had rows of pointed plates and spikes that shielded its body. The long sharp horns of *Triceratops* pointed forward from its head like deadly spears.

ANKYLOSAURUS

STEGOSAURUS

TRICERATOPS

How were smaller dinosaurs able to attack bigger ones?

Sometimes smaller flesh-eating dinosaurs hunted in groups. These groups could surround an old, slow dinosaur many times their size and close in for the kill.

DEINONYCHUS
(dy-NON-uh-kus)

SAUROLOPHUS
(sawr-AHL-uh-fus)

How tough was a *Tyrannosaurus*?

Many flesh-eating dinosaurs were fast and agile, bringing down prey several times their own weight. However, the huge, powerful jaws, the strong hind limbs, and—most important—the great size of *Tyrannosaurus* made the "tyrant" dinosaur the most terrifying flesh-eater that ever lived.

Why did *Tyrannosaurus* have such short, weak front legs?

Indeed the forelimbs were so short that *Tyrannosaurus* could not even reach its own mouth with them. No one knows exactly why this is so. It seems that as *Tyrannosaurus* evolved—developed over many generations— toward its large body size, its forelimbs got shorter and shorter.

Similar changes occur in each one of us during growth. When you were very young, your head was quite large compared to the rest of your body. But as you get older, your head becomes smaller compared to your body. Imagine if we grew to the size of *Tyrannosaurus*. We would have tiny heads and huge bodies.

What parts of *Tyrannosaurus* are most commonly found?

Paleontologists rarely find *Tyrannosaurus* skeletons. They usually find the huge fearsome teeth. This is because *Tyrannosaurus* regularly produced new teeth, as many living animals do. They replaced older, worn teeth that fell out of the jaws. With a mouth full of new teeth, *Tyrannosaurus* was always ready for a meal.

TYRANNOSAURUS

OVIRAPTOR

Another reason why teeth are found is that they are the hardest part of the body. When all the bones of a skeleton have been washed away by wind and rain, the teeth remain on the surface of the ground.

Why did *Tyrannosaurus* die out?

Near the end of the age of dinosaurs the climate changed. Winters became cooler, and summers became hotter. *Tyrannosaurus* and its dinosaur relatives were not comfortable in this new weather, and they could not survive in large numbers. Finally they died out.

Other animals were able to survive, such as the mouselike mammals with their covering of fur. These survivors from the age of dinosaurs developed into the animals that live today, including ourselves.

Are any animals alive today related to the dinosaurs?

Yes. The ancestry of birds can be traced back to small flesh-eating relatives of *Tyrannosaurus*. In the long view of time, birds are really feathered dinosaurs!